CATS
IN
CHAOS

For Snowy, our regular feline snack-hunter.

P.B.

For Nico.

J.B.

First published in the United Kingdom by HarperCollins *Children's Books* in 2022

HarperCollins *Children's Books* is a division of HarperCollins*Publishers* Ltd
1 London Bridge Street, London SE1 9GF

www.harpercollins.co.uk

HarperCollins*Publishers*
1st Floor, Watermarque Building, Ringsend Road, Dublin 4, Ireland

1 3 5 7 9 10 8 6 4 2

Text copyright © Peter Bently 2022
Illustrations copyright © John Bond 2022

ISBN: 978-0-00-846918-4

Printed in China

CATS
IN
CHAOS

BY PETER BENTLY
& JOHN BOND

HarperCollins *Children's Books*

CATS adore eating and snoozing and **SNUGGLING**. They also like acrobats, tightropes and **JUGGLING**.

They slip from their **houses** as soon as it's **DARK**

and head for the **school** by the side of the **PARK**.

Here's **MARMADUKE CATSBY**
to welcome them in:

**"ROLL UP!
ROLL UP!**

We're about to begin!

Prepare to be dazzled
and dazed with delight!
CATSBY'S GREAT CIRCUS
is in town
TONIGHT!"

To kick off the evening it's **WHISKERS O'FARRELL**.
She takes **careful aim** as she lines up the **BARREL**.

BOO

M!

See her SOARING!
But where will she LAND?

Inside the FISH SHOP!
How perfectly GRAND!

Then **KITTY KADABRA**, the conjuring cat, pulls a great string of **SAUSAGES** out of her **HAT!**

Some moggies run forward to wish her **"WELL DONE!"**

And the sausages magically
vanish, **EACH ONE!**

"OOPS!" declares CATSBY. "But now for a thrill! It's DAISY THE DOG TAMER next on the bill!"

The KITTENS cling on to their dads and their mums,

as into the ring an **ENORMOUS** pooch comes!

Daisy cries **"SIT!"** then,
to thunderous applause,

she sticks her
WHOLE HEAD
in the massive mutt's jaws!

But look! There's a **MOUSE!**

There are yowls of surprise.

That's not a **DOG** . . .

... it's just **CATS IN DISGUISE!**

Marmaduke shoos them away with a frown.

"The show must go on! Send in **KATNIP THE CLOWN!**"

The cats **LAUGH** so much they have tears in their eyes –
just look how he **juggles** with mackerel pies!

Three **PIES**   and four **PIES**   and five **PIES**

and **SIX!**

The mogs are amazed at his
marvellous **TRICKS** . . .

. . . while **THREE SIAMESE,**
with the greatest of ease,
do fabulous feats
on the flying trapeze.

They swing low!

They swing high!

See them spin!

See them fly!

See them all snatching a **MACKEREL PIE!**

IT'S CHAOS! thinks Catsby. He's looking quite vexed.
He hastily hollers, "So now folks, **WHO'S NEXT?**

Prepare to be gobsmacked as **PURRCULES CLAW**
balances thirty-one cats on one paw!"

But there goes that **MOUSE!**
It makes Purrcules stumble . . .
What a **CAT**-astrophe!
Down they all **TUMBLE!**

"PIPE DOWN!" cries Catsby. "It's time for a treat –
it's **EVEL KATNEVEL!** Hold on to your seat!"

"ME-OOH!"
cry the crowd and
"ME-AH!" and "WHOOP-WHOOP!"
as Evel flies in through a
great flaming **HOOP** . . .

Then he heads for a ramp that's
as high as you wish

and prepares to **JUMP** over . . .

. . . a **TRUCKLOAD OF FISH!**

VROOM!

Up the ramp speeds
the daredevil cat,
but – **OH NO!**
Just hold on a minute –
WHAT'S THAT?

It's the **MOUSE** once again!

Evel skids!

Evel swerves!

Catsby can't look –
it's too much for his nerves!

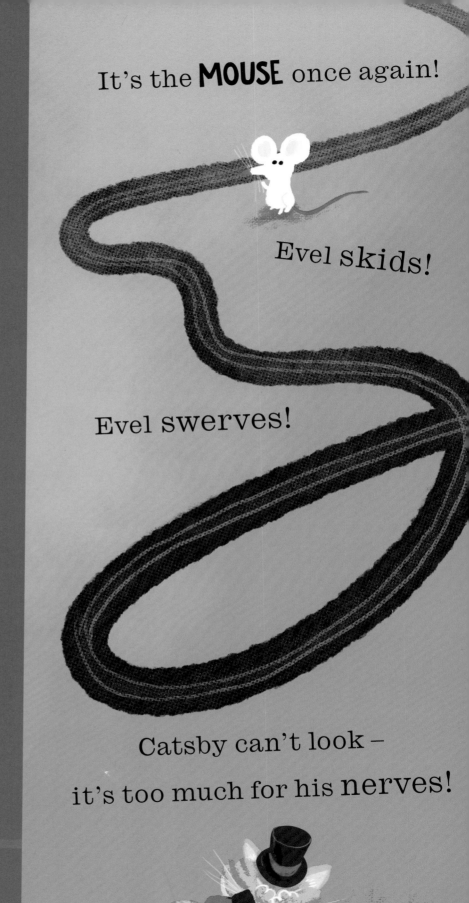

EVEL KATNEVEL heads straight for the **TRUCK.**

Then . . .

a Siamese swings down and grabs him!
WHAT LUCK!

The bike hurtles onward. It's going to **CRASH!**

It collides with the truck
with a massive great

SMASH!!!!

The fish crates lie **SHATTERED**. The cats can't stop staring . . .

at salmon   and codfish   and haddock

and herring.

HUNDREDS of cat brains are silently whirring.

The circus is filled with an ominous **PURRING** . . .

What follows next is a bit of a blur –
of **YOWLING** and **CHOMPING**
and fishes and fur . . .

"If you can't beat 'em, join 'em!"
cries **CATSBY** with glee.

"Chaos is fine
when there's
**FISH GOING
FREE!"**

Next morning, most moggies are still soundly **SNOOZING**.

They even missed **BREAKFAST**, which folks find confusing.

But some are up early. They don't want to **SNUGGLE**.

They're all in the garden shed . . .

...learning to **JUGGLE.**